NEW YORK REVIEW BOOKS
CLASSICS

CHESS STORY

STEFAN ZWEIG (1881–1942), novelist, biographer,
poet, and translator, was born in Vienna into a wealthy
Austrian-Jewish family. He studied at the Universities of
Berlin and Vienna. With the rise of Nazism, he moved
from Salzburg to London (taking British citizenship),
to New York, and finally to Brazil where he committed
suicide with his wife. Among his most celebrated books
are his memoir of the Vienna of his youth, *The World of
Yesterday*, and a novel, *Beware of Pity* (forthcoming from
NYRB Classics).

PETER GAY was born in Berlin in 1923 and emigrated
to the United States along with his family as a teenager.
He has written many works of social and intellectual history, including *The Enlightenment: An Interpretation*,
which won the National Book Award, *Schnitzler's
Century*, and several studies of Freud. He is Sterling
Professor of History Emeritus at Yale University.

CHESS STORY

STEFAN ZWEIG

Translated from the German by
JOEL ROTENBERG

Introduction by
PETER GAY

NEW YORK REVIEW BOOKS

New York

THIS IS A NEW YORK REVIEW BOOK
PUBLISHED BY THE NEW YORK REVIEW OF BOOKS
435 Hudson Street, New York, NY 10014
www.nyrb.com

Published in the German language as *Schachnovelle*

Zweig, Stefan, 1881–1942.
  [Schachnovelle. English]
  Chess story / by Stefan Zweig ; translation by Joel Rotenberg.
      p. cm. — (New York Review Books classics)
  ISBN 1-59017-169-1 (alk. paper)
  I. Rotenberg, Joel. II. Title. III. Series.
  PT2653.W42S3513 2005
  833'.912—dc22

                                    2005012029

ISBN 978-1-59017-169-1
Available as an electronic book; ISBN 978-1-59017-560-6

Printed in the United States of America on acid-free paper.
1 0

INTRODUCTION

STEFAN Zweig was one of Hitler's posthumous victims. Born in Vienna in November 1881, the son of a rich Jewish textile manufacturer, he began his writer's life as a poet. His first book was a collection of lyrical verse, *Silberne Saiten* (*Silver Strings*, 1901), which taught him that his proper activity lay in the domain of prose. Zweig wrote constantly and easily, in a variety of genres. He translated French literature. In 1935, he wrote the libretto for an opera, *Die Schweig-same Frau* (*The Silent Woman*), by Richard Strauss (who after the death of Hugo von Hofmannsthal was in desperate search for a new librettist and had no compunction about working with the Jew Zweig). He published biographical profiles both short and long. He wrote novellas and novels. In 1919, after the First World War, he settled in picturesque Salzburg, Mozart's unloved hometown, writing. In 1935, antici-pating the Nazis' takeover of Austria by three years, he emigrated to England, only to move, in 1940, to Brazil. It was there, in February 1942, that he com-mitted suicide, as did his wife. Zweig left behind, among other works, an unfinished essay on Balzac, an autobiography, *Die Welt von Gestern* (*The World of Yesterday*), and a novella, *Schachnovelle*, here translated as *Chess Story*, both to be published soon after his death. "He died," wrote the novelist and editor Hermann Kesten, one of the "good" Germans, "like a philosopher."

Alive or dead, Stefan Zweig was, and to a significant degree still is, an unfailingly popular writer mainly, but by no means only, in the German-speaking world. The text I have been working with, a Fisher paperback dated December 2004, is in its fifty-second printing, an astonishing record that attests to his lasting appeal. His novellas and biographical essays, the two solid foundations of his enduring reputation, are seductive in their celebrated style, invariably casual and informal in tone, shrewd in their choice of themes, and, in the best sense of the term, conventional.

Zweig's last writings were consistent with the work he had been doing for decades. The essay on Balzac is characteristic of him, the last in a substantial series of biographical sketches and historical portraits, in which he tried to nail down the essence of a figure that interested him: Casanova, Tolstoy, Dostoyevsky, Hölderlin, Erasmus, and Mary Queen of Scots. They are psychological forays in which Zweig attempted to

dig beneath the surface, beyond superficial appearance to inner reality, to intellectual and emotional
responses of personages whose political and cultural
qualities seemed worth exploring. Their lives led
Zweig to place them into, or against, their culture.
His Dickens is at home among unfailingly compla-
cent and prudish Victorians, and his Nietzsche is
an isolated truth-teller not at home anywhere. We
can still read these agreeable essays with pleasure and
profit, though Zweig's strongly felt need to find a
dominant trait—reminiscent of his great favorite,
Balzac—often makes them more ingenious than
precise.

That this self-confident proceeding was risky
emerges plainly from his autobiography, *The World
of Yesterday.* It is chatty and hyperbolic, brilliantly
capturing prominent elements in his pre–World War
bourgeois culture but setting aside cogent evidence
that might contradict, or at least complicate, his
generalizations. Thus—to give a telling example—
Zweig's account of young women in respectable
Viennese society before 1914 amounts to a single-
minded assault on middle-class family life that is quite
one-sided. He writes about overprotected maidens
who were kept "in a completely sterilized atmos-
phere," innocents who became "educated and over-
educated," for the most part "foolish and untaught,

well-bred and unsuspecting, inquisitive and shy, uncertain and impractical, and predetermined by this unworldly education to be shaped and led in marriage by their husbands without a will of their own." To Zweig's vision, both penetrating but also rather myopic, sex was taboo for unmarried females not only as an activity before marriage but also as a subject of conversation.

This deplorable state of affairs, to which Zweig chose to devote ample space, could doubtless have been observed among some, perhaps even many, of the young ladies of his acquaintance, but there were other Viennese bourgeoises in his time who worked sturdily toward revising, even eliminating, these attitudes, whether as feminists, university students, or intrepid philanthropists. Of course, when Zweig came to write his autobiography, his liberal culture which he remembered fondly but not uncritically, had been destroyed, and, in retrospect, Zweig saw his past—so distant now!—with a storyteller's clarity that was overstated for the sake of a literary point. Real life was usually more nuanced than Zweig was ready to acknowledge.

But in his *Chess Story*—an effective, terse fiction that is among his most successful—Zweig a little indirectly confronted the horrors of his own time, about which he had long remained silent. Chess, a game however noble—it is not called the "royal game" for nothing—becomes in his hands a double duel: a life-and-death struggle between Mirko Czentovic, the world champion, and an aggressive challenger, an amateur, the moody Scottish engineer, McConnor; more importantly, though, the duel is between Czentovic and a certain Dr. B., an Austrian lawyer of Royalist sympathies, taken prisoner by the Gestapo in March 1938, as the Nazis invaded Austria, and for long months held in solitary confinement while being subjected to relentless interrogation. We learn from the story that by a lucky accident, a chess manual fell into Dr. B's hands, for a while alleviating the burden of his isolation, and that by playing and replaying chess in his head he mastered the game, only to be driven out of his mind by the strange exercise of functioning as his own opponent. Now released from captivity and allowed to go into exile, Dr. B. retains his striking and strangely acquired competence as a chess player, which turns out to have a crucial bearing on the struggle between Czentovic and McConnor. As usual in Zweig's fiction, separate strands of a complex plot overlap and blend into one.

Indeed, *Chess Story* beautifully exhibits the private strategy that lies at the heart of Zweig's literary labors, especially in his novellas and his biographical sketches. He might oversimplify his tale to accommodate a sweeping aphorism or a dramatic conclusion, but he always saw himself as a detective whose principal task it was, whether he was writing fiction or nonfiction, to unriddle the mystery that shaped the life of a Dostoyevsky or a Hölderlin, a Czentovic or a Dr. B. And to clothe his discoveries in eminently readable prose.

It should surprise nobody that Zweig was an occasional correspondent of Freud's, dedicated a collection of biographical essays to him, and thought of himself as Freud's ally in the great venture of understanding human nature. In 1929, Zweig a little effusively told Freud how highly he thought of psychoanalysis:

> I believe that the revolution you have called forth in the psychological and philosophical and the whole moral structure of our world greatly outweighs the merely therapeutic part of your discoveries. For today all the people who know nothing about you, every human being of 1930, even the one who had never heard the name of psychoanalyst, is already indirectly dyed through and through by your transformation of souls.

The very extravagance of Zweig's admiration for Freud eloquently attests to his own aspiration to be the psychologist to his culture. In return, Freud's enthusiasm for Stefan Zweig's work may have been a little excessive. He declared Zweig a "personal friend" and his novella, *Vierundzwanzig Stunden aus dem Leben einer Frau* (*Twenty-four Hours in the Life of a Woman,* 1927), which closely resembles *Chess Story,* a "little masterpiece." Zweig's analyses were not quite psychoanalyses, but the characters he so freely invented in his fictions often seem like the subjects of gracefully presented case histories.

Without literally repeating himself, Zweig frequently turned in his novellas to a narrative device—a form of presentation he might have patented, he employed it so frequently—that I might call a secondary narrator. He tends to enforce the intimacy of his "case histories" by resorting to a first-person narrator and at the same time keep this intimacy under control by having the events of his tale largely presented by a third person, who exploits the narrator as the recipient of a fascinating tale.

In *Chess Story,* Zweig uses this distancing technique twice. In relating the background and the education of Mirko Czentovic who, as a kind of idiot savant, is ignorant of everything except chess, he employs a friend of the main narrator to fill in the indispensable details. And then, later in the novella, he has Dr. B. tell the narrator the story of his terrible schooling in chess by the Nazi conquerors of Austria. This crucial story oddly parallels the information the narrator had received about Czentovic's apprenticeship: there is more than one way of growing into a master chess player. And this echo underscores Zweig's indirect manner of getting the story underway and keeping it alive through the denouement. It permits him to be at once revelatory and discreet. He can be as liberal as he wishes to be, and no more.

A look at Zweig's *Twenty-four Hours in the Life of a Woman*, the one that Freud called a "little masterpiece," should clarify his use of this technique of the secondary narrator. A distinguished widow in her early forties who has remained faithful to the memory of her late husband, on holiday in Monte Carlo, visits the casino and is fascinated by the sight of a young gambler's hands. He is handsome, the age of the lady's elder son. As he leaves the casino in despair, having lost a great deal of money, and possibly intending to kill himself, she follows him and tries to save him. She talks to him, gives him money, goes to his room, eventually spending the night with him, having exacted his guarantee not to gamble anymore. She promises to say goodbye to him at the railway station but misses his train. She then make a final visit to the casino, where once again she catches sight of the gambler's hands. She reproaches him angrily and he throws at her the money she had given him for the trip home. The novella does not end until Zweig lets the reader know that her mission had failed: the young man committed suicide.

The narrator does not expound the story directly; rather, he visits the lady at her invitation and she volunteers the story of her fateful twenty-four hours. In a paper of 1927, "Dostoyevsky and Parricide," Freud praised the story for being "brilliantly told, faultlessly motivated," but he also acknowledged that it was not a psychoanalytic story—Zweig had, to Freud's mind, laid out the motives of all the actors "faultlessly," but had concealed these motives from himself as well as his readers. Freud also recognized that the "*façade* given to the story by its author"—the secondary narrator—"seeks to disguise its analytic meaning." By having the reputable middle-aged woman pour out her tale, which the narrator then retells as he was told it, the author and his narrator both stand protected. The lady, who has been excessively frank about all sorts of intimate physical and psychological details, refuses to tell him whether she and the stranger whose life she had wished to save made love. Freud, in summarizing *Twenty-four Hours in the Life of a Woman*, obviously thinks that they have. But the text is equivocal, and Zweig avoids fully disclosing an oedipal entanglement of mother and son that Freud sees as his true subject. Thus Zweig draws a last veil of reserve over his story, which is anything but a case history.

This reserve haunts *Chess Story* as well. The author tells his readers through his primary narrator that Dr. B., who has become the principal figure in the novella, "would never again touch a chessboard." Is that all? Will he eventually deal with his trauma and live, or, like Stefan Zweig, defeated by exile and depression, let his past conquer him and die? We know that Zweig's world, the liberal culture of Central Europe, was no more; for a writer who could always count on a sizable and admiring audience, this was an ordeal hard to acknowledge and hard to survive. Before the all-too-final act of suicide, Zweig, writing *Chess Story*, might have included his readers more frankly, more openly, about the desperate struggles within him. But his discretion, so typical for him, kept him from such confessional candor. It is as though *Chess Story* is a message from an earlier age, from the World of Yesterday.

—PETER GAY

CHESS STORY

ON THE great passenger steamer, due to depart New York for Buenos Aires at midnight, there was the usual last-minute bustle and commotion. Visitors from shore shoved confusedly to see their friends off, telegraph boys in cocked caps dashed through the lounges shouting names, trunks and flowers were carried past, and inquisitive children ran up and down the companionways, the orchestra playing imperturbably on deck all the while. As I was standing a bit apart from this hubbub, talking on the promenade deck with an acquaintance of mine, two or three flashbulbs flared near us—apparently the press had been quickly interviewing and photographing some celebrity just before we sailed. My friend glanced over and smiled. "That's a rare bird you've got on board—that's Czentovic." I must have received this news with a rather blank look, for he went on to explain, "Mirko Czentovic, the world chess champion. He's crisscrossed America from coast to coast playing tournaments and is now off to Argentina for fresh triumphs."

In fact I now recalled this young world champion and even some details of his meteoric career; my friend, a more assiduous reader of newspapers than I, was able to add a number of anecdotes. About a year previously Czentovic had overnight entered the ranks of the greatest masters of the art of chess, such as Alekhine, Capablanca, Tartakower, Lasker, and Bogoljubov. Not since the appearance of the seven-year-old prodigy Reshevsky at the New York chess tournament of 1922 had the penetration of a complete unknown into that circle of luminaries caused such a wide sensation. For Czentovic's intellectual traits certainly did not seem to promise a dazzling career. It soon emerged that, chess champion or not, in private Czentovic was unable to write a correctly spelled sentence in any language, and, as one of his irritated peers gibed, "his ignorance was just as absolute in every other area."

Czentovic's father, a penniless Yugoslavian Danube bargeman, had been killed in his tiny boat when it was crushed one night by a grain steamer in a remote area; the twelve-year-old boy had then been taken in by the local parson out of pity. The good reverend coached him at home, doing his level best to make up for what the lumpish, taciturn, broad-browed boy was unable to learn at the village school.

But the parson's efforts were in vain. The letters of

the alphabet had been explained to the boy a hundred times, yet still he stared at them as though he had never seen them before; no matter how simple the subject, his brain labored heavily but retained nothing. At the age of fourteen he still counted on his fingers, and, though he was now an adolescent, he could read books and newspapers only with great difficulty. Yet Mirko could not be called reluctant or willful. He obediently did what was asked, carried water, split wood, helped in the fields, cleaned the kitchen, and reliably (though with annoying slowness) finished any task he was given. But what irritated the good parson most about the awkward boy was his total apathy. He did nothing unless specifically told to, never asked a question, did not play with other boys, and undertook no activity that had not been explicitly assigned to him; once Mirko had finished his chores, he sat around listlessly indoors with the vacant look of sheep at pasture, taking not the slightest interest in what went on around him. While the parson, puffing on his long peasant pipe, played his usual three evening games of chess with the local constable, the lank-haired blond boy squatted silently beside them and gazed at the checkered board from beneath his heavy eyelids, seemingly somnolent and indifferent.

One winter evening while the two players were

engrossed in their daily game, the jingle of sleigh bells came from the village street, approaching with greater and greater speed. A peasant, his cap dusted with snow, stumped in hurriedly—his old mother was dying, and he wanted the parson to hurry so that he would be in time to administer the last rites. The parson followed without hesitation. As he was leaving, the constable, who was still drinking his beer, lit a fresh pipe and was preparing to pull on his heavy top boots when he noticed that Mirko's gaze was riveted on the chessboard with the unfinished game.

"So, you want to play it out, do you?" he said jokingly, completely convinced that the sleepy boy did not know how to move a single piece on the board correctly. The boy looked up shyly, then nodded and took the parson's chair. After fourteen moves the constable had been beaten, and, he had to admit, through no careless error of his own. The second game ended no differently.

"Balaam's ass!" exclaimed the astounded parson upon his return, explaining to the constable, who was not so well versed in the Bible, that by a similar miracle two thousand years ago a dumb creature had suddenly found the power of intelligent speech. In spite of the late hour, the parson could not refrain from challenging his semiliterate famulus. Mirko beat him too with ease. He played doggedly, slowly, stolidly, without once lifting his bowed broad forehead from the board. But he played with unassailable certainty; during the days to come neither the constable nor the parson was able to win a game against him. The parson, who knew better than anyone how backward his pupil was in other respects, now became curious in earnest as to how far this one strange talent might withstand a more rigorous test. After having Mirko's unkempt blond hair cut at the village barber's, to make him somewhat presentable, he took him in his sleigh to the small neighboring city where, in a corner of the café in the main square, there were chess enthusiasts for whom (as he had found) he himself was no match. There was no small stir among them when the parson pushed the tow-headed, rosy-cheeked fifteen-year-old in his fur-lined sheepskin jacket and heavy, high-top boots into the coffeehouse, where, ill at ease, the boy stood in a corner with shyly downcast eyes until someone called him over to one of the chess tables. Mirko lost against his first opponent, because he had never seen the "Sicilian opening" in the good parson's game. He drew the second game, against the best player. From the third and fourth games on, he beat all his opponents, one after another.

Now it is rare indeed that anything exciting happens in a small provincial city in Yugoslavia, and the first appearance of this rustic champion caused an instant sensation among those in attendance. There was unanimous agreement that the boy wonder must definitely remain in the city until the next day, so that the other members of the chess club could be assembled and especially so that old Count Simczic, a chess fanatic, could be reached at his castle. The parson looked at his ward with a pride that was quite new, but, for all his joy of discovery, he still did not wish to neglect his duty to perform the Sunday services; he declared himself willing to leave Mirko behind for a further test. The young Czentovic was put up in the hotel at the chess club's expense and saw a water closet that evening for the first time. The next afternoon, the chess room in the café was jammed. Mirko, sitting motionless in front of the board for four hours, defeated one player after another without uttering a word or even looking up; finally a simultaneous game was proposed. It took some time to make the ignorant boy understand that in a simultaneous game he would be the only opponent of a range of players. But once Mirko had grasped this, he quickly warmed to the task. He moved slowly from table to table, his heavy shoes squeaking, and in the end won seven of the eight games.

At this point great deliberations began. Although this new champion was not strictly speaking a resident, regional pride was keenly aroused just the same. Perhaps the small city, whose presence on the map had hardly ever been noticed, could finally boast of an international celebrity. An agent by the name of Koller, who otherwise represented nobody but chanteuses and cabaret singers employed at the garrison, announced that, in return for a year's subsidy, he would arrange to have the young man given professional training in the art of chess by an excellent minor master of his acquaintance in Vienna. Count Simczic, who in sixty years of daily play had never encountered such a remarkable opponent, immediately underwrote the amount. That day marked the beginning of the astonishing career of the boatman's son.

After half a year Mirko had mastered all the secrets of chess technique, though with a peculiar limitation that was later to be much noted and ridiculed in professional circles. For Czentovic never managed to play a single game by memory alone—"blind," as the professionals say. He completely lacked the ability to situate the field of battle in the unlimited realm of the imagination. He always needed to have the board with its sixty-four black and white squares and thirty-two pieces physically in front of him; even when he was world-famous, he carried a folding pocket chess set with him at all times so that, if he wanted to reconstruct a game or solve a problem, he would be able to examine the positions of the pieces by eye. This failing, in itself minor, betrayed a lack of imaginative power and was the subject of lively discussion in elite circles, of the sort that might be heard among musicians if a prominent virtuoso or conductor had proven himself unable to play or conduct without an open score. But this strange idiosyncrasy did nothing whatever to slow Mirko's stupendous climb. At seventeen he had already won a dozen prizes, at eighteen the Hungarian Championship, and at twenty he was champion of the world. The most audacious grandmasters, every one of them infinitely superior to him in intellectual gifts, imagination, and daring, fell to his cold and inexorable logic as Napoleon to the ponderous Kutuzov or Hannibal to Fabius Cunctator (who, according to Livy's report, displayed similar conspicuous traits of phlegm and imbecility in childhood). Thus it happened that the illustrious gallery of chess champions, including among their number the most varied types of superior intellect—philosophers, mathematicians, people whose natural talents were computational, imaginative, often creative—was for the first time invaded by a total outsider to the intellectual world, a dull, taciturn peasant lad, from whom even the craftiest newspapermen were never able to coax a single word of any journalistic value. Of course, what Czentovic denied the newspapers in the way of polished sentences was soon amply compensated for in anecdotes about his person. For the instant he stood up from the chessboard, where he was without peer, Czentovic became an irredeemably grotesque, almost comic figure; despite his solemn black suit, his splendid cravat with its somewhat showy pearl stickpin, and his painstakingly manicured fingernails, his behavior and manners remained those of the simple country boy who had once swept out the parson's room in the village. To the amusement and annoyance of his professional peers, he was artless and almost brazen in extracting, with a miserly, even vulgar greed, what money he could from his talent and fame. He traveled from city to city, always staying in the cheapest hotels, he played in the most pathetic clubs as long as they paid his fee, he permitted himself to appear in soap advertisements, and even—ignoring the mockery of his competitors, who knew quite well that he couldn't put three sentences together—sold his name for use on the cover of a *Philosophy of Chess* which had actually been written for the enterprising publisher by an insignificant Galician student. Like all headstrong types, Czentovic had no sense of the ridiculous; ever since his triumph in the world tournament, he considered himself the most important man in the world, and the awareness that he had beaten all these clever, intellectual, brilliant speakers and writers on their own ground, and above all the evident fact that he made more money than they did, transformed his original lack of self-confidence into a cold pride that for the most part he did not trouble to hide.

"But why wouldn't such a rapid rise to fame send an empty head like that into a spin?" concluded my friend, who had just related some classic examples of Czentovic's childishly authoritative manner. "Why wouldn't a twenty-one-year-old country boy from the Banat start putting on airs when pushing some pieces around on a wooden board is suddenly earning him more in a week than his whole village back home makes in an entire year of woodcutting and the most backbreaking drudgery? And, actually, isn't it damn easy to think you're a great man if you aren't troubled by the slightest notion that a Rembrandt, Beethoven, Dante, or Napoleon ever existed? This lad has just one piece of knowledge in his blinkered brain—that he hasn't lost a single chess game in months—and since he has no idea that there's anything of value in the world other than chess and money, he has every reason to be pleased with himself."

My friend's observations did not fail to arouse a special curiosity in me. All my life I have been passionately interested in monomaniacs of any kind, people carried away by a single idea. The more one limits oneself, the closer one is to the infinite; these people, as unworldly as they seem, burrow like termites into their own particular material to construct, in miniature, a strange and utterly individual image of the world. Thus I made no secret of my intention to subject this odd specimen of a one-track mind to a closer examination during the twelve-day voyage to Rio.

But my friend warned: "You won't have much luck. As far as I know, no one has yet succeeded in getting anything of the slightest psychological interest out of Czentovic. That wily peasant is tremendously shrewd behind all his abysmal limitations. He never lets anything slip—thanks to the simple technique of avoiding all conversation except with compatriots of his from the same walk of life, people he finds in small hotels. When he senses an educated person he crawls into his shell. That way no one will ever be able to boast of having heard him say something stupid or of having plumbed the depths of his seemingly boundless ignorance."

And in fact my friend would turn out to be right. During the first few days of the voyage it proved to be entirely impossible to approach Czentovic short of roughly thrusting myself upon him, which all things considered is not in my line. He did sometimes stride across the promenade deck, but always with a bearing of proud self-absorption, hands clasped behind him, like Napoleon in the famous pose; then too he always made his tour of the deck so hurriedly and propulsively that it would have been necessary to pursue him at a trot in order to accost him. Nor did he ever show himself in the lounges, the bar, or the smoking room; as the steward informed me in response to a discreet inquiry, he spent the greater part of the day in his cabin, practicing or reviewing chess games on a bulky board.

After three days I was beginning to be truly annoyed that his dogged defenses were outmaneuvering my determination to get near him. I had never in my life had an opportunity to make the personal acquaintance of a chess champion, and the more I now sought to form an impression of such a temperament, the more unimaginable appeared to me a mind absorbed for a lifetime in a domain of sixty-four black and white squares. From my own experience I was well aware of the mysterious attraction of the "royal game," which, alone among the games devised by man, regally eschews the tyranny of chance and awards its palms of victory only to the intellect, or rather to a certain type of intellectual gift. But is it not already an insult to call chess anything so narrow as a game? Is it not also a science, an art, hovering between these categories like Muhammad's coffin between heaven and earth, a unique yoking of opposites, ancient and yet eternally new, mechanically constituted and yet an activity of the imagination alone, limited to a fixed geometric area but unlimited in its permutations, constantly evolving and yet sterile, a cogitation producing nothing, a mathematics calculating nothing, an art without an artwork, an architecture without substance and yet demonstrably more durable in its essence and actual form than all books and works, the only game that belongs to all peoples and all eras, while no one knows what god put it on earth to deaden boredom, sharpen the mind, and fortify the spirit? Where does it begin, where does it end? Any child can learn its basic rules, any amateur can try his hand at it; and yet, within the inalterable confines of a chessboard, masters unlike any others evolve, people with a talent for chess and chess alone, special geniuses whose gifts of imagination, patience and skill are just as precisely apportioned as those of mathematicians, poets, and musicians, but differently arranged and combined. In earlier times, when there was a rage for physiognomy, a Gall might have dissected the brains of such chess champions to determine whether there was a special convolution in their gray matter, a kind of chess muscle or chess bump more strongly marked than in the skulls of others. And how excited such a physiognomist would have been by the case of a Czentovic, in whom this narrow genius seems embedded in absolute intellectual inertia like a single gold thread in a hundredweight of barren rock. In principle I have always found it easy to understand that such a unique, ingenious game would have to produce its own wizards. Yet how difficult, how impossible it is to imagine the life of an intellectually active person who reduces the world to a shuttle between black and white, who seeks fulfillment in a mere to-and-fro, forward-and-back of thirty-two pieces, someone for whom a new opening that allows the knight to be advanced instead of the pawn is in itself a great accomplishment and a meager little piece of immortality in a corner of a chess book—someone, someone with a brain in his head, who, without going mad, continues over and over for ten, twenty, thirty, forty years to devote all the force of his thought to the ridiculous end of cornering a wooden king on a wooden board!

And now that one such phenomenon, one such strange genius or mysterious simpleton was for the first time physically quite nearby, six cabins away from me on the same ship, alas! I, for whom curiosity about things of the mind is more and more becoming a kind of passion, was unable to approach him. I began to think up the most absurd ruses: I would tickle his vanity by pretending to interview him for an important newspaper, perhaps; or pique his avarice by proposing a lucrative tournament in Scotland. But finally I remembered a hunter's trick, that the most reliable technique for decoying the wood grouse was to imitate its mating call. What could be more effective in attracting the attention of a chess champion than to play chess oneself?

Now I have never in my life been a serious chess player; my dealings with the game have been purely frivolous, for pleasure alone. If I spend an hour in front of the board, this is by no means to exert myself but, on the contrary, to relieve emotional tension. I "play" chess in the truest sense, while the others, the real chess players, "work" it, if I may use the word in this daring new way. But, in chess as in love, a partner is indispensable, and at that time I did not yet know if there were other chess lovers on board apart from us. To lure them out of their holes, I laid a primitive trap in the smoking room. Though my wife's game is even weaker than my own, she and I, the bird-catchers, sat at a chessboard. And in fact someone passing through paused for a moment before we had made even six moves and a second asked permission to look on; finally the desired partner turned up too, and challenged me to a game. His name was McConnor, a Scottish civil engineer who, as I soon heard, had made a fortune in oil drilling in California. To the eye he was a thickset individual with heavy, well-defined, almost rectilinear jowls, strong teeth, and a high complexion whose pronounced ruddiness was probably at least partly due to plenty of whisky. The strikingly broad, almost athletically powerful shoulders unfortunately reflected the character of his playing too, for this Mr. McConnor was one of those self-obsessed big wheels who feel personally diminished by a defeat in even the most trivial game. Accustomed to ruthlessly asserting himself in life and spoiled by actual success, this unyielding self-made man was so unshakably imbued with a sense of his own superiority that any resistance infuriated him, as though it were some inadmissible revolt, practically an affront. When he lost the first game, he grew sullen and began proclaiming, dictatorially and longwindedly, that this could only have happened because his attention had wandered for a moment; he blamed his failure in the third game on noise from the next room. He was unable to lose without immediately demanding a return match. At first I was amused by this dogged pride; finally I accepted it as an unavoidable side effect of my real purpose, to lure the world champion to our table.

On the third day the plan succeeded, or partly. Whether Czentovic had looked through the porthole on the promenade deck and seen us in front of the chessboard or had just happened to honor the smoking room with his presence—in any event, as soon as he saw two incompetents practicing his art, he was compelled to step closer and while maintaining a careful distance cast an appraising glance at our board. McConnor was just then making a move. And even this one move seemed to be enough to tell Czentovic that it would be unworthy of a master like him to take any further interest in our amateurish efforts. As naturally as any of us might toss aside a bad detective novel in a bookstore without even opening it, he walked away from our table and out of the smoking room. "Weighed in the balance and found wanting," I thought, a little annoyed by this cool, contemptuous gaze; to somehow give vent to my ill-humor, I said to McConnor:

"The champion didn't seem to think much of your move."

"What champion?"

I explained to him that the gentleman who had just passed by and looked with such disapproval at our game was the chess champion Czentovic. Well, I added, the two of us would get over it, we'd come to terms with his lofty contempt without heartache; beggars couldn't be choosers. But my offhand remark had a surprising and completely unexpected effect on

McConnor. He immediately became agitated and forgot our game; you could almost hear the throbbing of his pride. He had had no idea that Czentovic was on board. Czentovic absolutely had to play him. He had never in his life played against a world champion except once in a simultaneous game with forty others; even that had been terribly exciting, and he had almost won. Did I know the champion personally? I said I didn't. Wouldn't I talk to him and ask him over? I refused on the grounds that, to the best of my knowledge, Czentovic was not very open to making new acquaintances. Besides, what would tempt a world champion to bother with third-rate players like us?

Now I should never have made that remark about third-rate players to someone as proud as McConnor. He sat back in anger and brusquely declared that he for his part could not believe that Czentovic would refuse an invitation from a gentleman; he would see to that. At his request I provided him with a brief description of the world champion, and, abandoning our board, he rushed after Czentovic along the promenade deck with unbridled impatience. I felt again that anyone with such broad shoulders was not to be deterred once he had put his mind to something.

I waited in some anxiety. After ten minutes,

McConnor returned. He was not in good spirits, it seemed to me.

"Well?" I asked.

"You were right," he responded, with some annoyance. "Not a very pleasant gentleman. I introduced myself, told him who I was. He didn't even care to shake hands. I tried to explain to him how honored and proud all of us here on board would be if he would play us in a simultaneous game. But he was damn stiff-necked about it; said he was sorry, but he had contractual obligations toward his agent expressly prohibiting him from playing without a fee during his tour. He says his minimum is two hundred fifty dollars a game."

I laughed. "Who would have thought that pushing black and white pieces around was such a lucrative business. Well, I hope you took your leave just as politely."

But McConnor was deadly earnest. "The game is set for tomorrow afternoon at three. Here in the smoking lounge. I hope we won't let ourselves be thrashed too easily."

"What? You gave him two hundred fifty dollars?" I exclaimed in consternation.

"Why not? *C'est son métier.* If I had a toothache and there happened to be a dentist on board, I wouldn't ask him to pull my tooth free of charge.

The man is quite right to set hefty prices; in every field, the real experts are also the best at business. And as far as I'm concerned, the more straightforward the deal, the better. I'd rather pay cash than have Mr. Czentovic do me a favor and be obliged to him. Anyway, I've lost more than two hundred fifty dollars in an evening at our club, and I wasn't playing a world champion. For 'third-rate' players it's no disgrace to be flattened by a Czentovic."

I was amused to see how deeply I had wounded McConnor's self-esteem with that single innocent phrase "third-rate player." But as he was of a mind to pay for the expensive business, I wasn't about to find fault with his misplaced pride, which would enable me to meet the object of my curiosity at last. We lost no time in informing the four or five gentlemen who had identified themselves as chess players of the impending event, and, in advance of the match, we reserved not only our table but the adjoining ones too so as to minimize any disruption by people passing through.

The next day our little group turned out at the appointed hour in full strength. The central seat, opposite the champion, was of course assigned to McConnor, who eased his nerves by lighting one strong cigar after another and restlessly checking the time again and again. But the world champion kept

us waiting for a good ten minutes (I had had a pre-
sentiment of something of the kind from my friend's
tales), which only heightened the effect of his poised
entrance. He walked calmly and coolly to the table.
Without introducing himself—"You know who I
am, and who you are is of no interest to me," this
rudeness seemed to say—he embarked with professional dryness on the technical arrangements. As the
unavailability of chessboards on the ship made a simultaneous game impossible, he said, he proposed to
play us all jointly. After each move he would repair
to a table at the other end of the room in order not to
disturb our consultations. Once we had made our
own move, we would tap on a glass with a spoon
(unfortunately we didn't have a bell). He suggested a
ten-minute maximum for a move, unless we had another thought. Like bashful schoolboys we agreed to
everything. Czentovic drew black; he made the first
countermove while still on his feet and immediately
went to wait in the spot he had suggested, where, casually hunched over, he leafed through an illustrated
magazine.

There is little reason to describe the game. It
ended, as it had to, in our total defeat, after only
twenty-four moves. In and of itself it was hardly surprising that a world chess champion had dispatched
a half-dozen average or below-average players with

his left hand; what was so depressing to us was the overpowering way in which Czentovic made us feel all too clearly that he was doing just that. He would cast a single, seemingly cursory glance at the board before each move, looking past us as indifferently as if we ourselves were lifeless wooden pieces. It was a rude gesture that irresistibly recalled someone averting his eyes while tossing a scrap to a mangy dog. With a bit of sensitivity he could have drawn our attention to mistakes or bucked us up with a friendly word, in my opinion. But even when the game was over, this chess automaton uttered not a syllable after saying "mate," but simply waited motionless in front of the board in case we wanted a second game. I had already stood up—clumsy as one always is when faced with crass bad manners—in an attempt to indicate that, with the conclusion of this cash transaction, the pleasure of our acquaintance was at an end, at least as far as I was concerned. But to my annoyance I heard the rather hoarse voice of McConnor next to me: "Rematch!"

The sheer provocation in his tone startled me; in fact McConnor at that moment looked more like a boxer about to throw a punch than a polite gentleman. Whether because of Czentovic's unpleasant behavior or merely his own pathologically touchy pride, McConnor was in any case completely changed. Red to the roots of his hair, nostrils flared with the strength of his feeling, he was perspiring visibly, and a sharp crease ran between his firmly set lips and his aggressively jutting chin. I recognized uneasily in his eyes that flicker of uncontrolled passion that for the most part only grips people when they are at the roulette table and the right color hasn't come up six or seven times running, the stakes doubling and redoubling all the while. At that instant I knew that, regardless of the stakes, this fanatically proud man would go on playing Czentovic until he had won at least once, even if it cost him his entire fortune. If Czentovic stuck it out, he had found in McConnor a gold mine from which he could shovel dollars by the thousands all the way to Buenos Aires.

Czentovic remained impassive. "As you wish," he responded politely. "The gentlemen will now play black."

The second game went much as the first, except that some curious onlookers both swelled and enlivened our group. McConnor gazed so fixedly at the board that it was as if he was trying to magnetize the pieces with his will to win; I knew that he would happily have sacrificed even a thousand dollars for the pleasure of shouting "Mate!" at his heartless adversary. Strange to say, we were all unconsciously picking up some of his determined agitation. We discussed each move with much greater passion than before, restraining each other until the last minute before agreeing to give the signal that summoned Czentovic back to our table. Little by little we had arrived at the thirty-seventh move, and to our own surprise our position seemed amazingly advantageous, because we had succeeded in advancing the pawn in file c to the penultimate square c2; we needed only to move it to c1 to win a new queen. Not that we were smug about this all too obvious opportunity; we were unanimous in suspecting that this apparent advantage must be a trap set by Czentovic, who did after all have a much broader view of the situation. But despite strenuous general study and discussion we were unable to discover the subterfuge. Finally, just as our time was expiring, we decided to risk it. McConnor had his hand on the pawn to move it to the last square when he felt his arm abruptly seized, and someone said in a faint, urgent whisper: "For God's sake! Don't!"

Involuntarily we all turned. It was a gentleman of about forty-five, whose long, sharp-featured face and strange, almost chalky pallor had caught my attention on the promenade deck. He must have come up during the last few minutes while all our attention was on our problem. Feeling our gaze upon him, he added quickly:

"If you make a queen now, he'll take her immediately with bishop to c1, and you'll take his bishop with your knight. But he'll be moving his free pawn to d7 to threaten your rook, and even if you check with your knight you'll lose—you'll be done for in nine or ten moves. It's almost the same as the combination that Alekhine introduced against Bogoljubov in the Pistyan Grand Tournament of 1922."

Astonished, McConnor let his hand drop from the piece and stared with no less awe than the rest of us at the man who had unexpectedly come to our aid like an angel from heaven. Anyone who could calculate a checkmate nine moves ahead had to be an expert of the first rank, perhaps even a competitor for the championship traveling to the same tournament. There was something supernatural about his sudden appearance and intervention at such a critical juncture. McConnor was the first to recover his wits.

"What would you advise?" he whispered excitedly.

"Don't advance just yet, first take evasive action! The main thing is to move your king out of the endangered file, from g8 to h7. Then he'll probably shift his attack to the other flank. But you can parry that with rook c8–c4; that will cost him two tempi, a pawn, and thus his advantage. Then it'll be your free pawn against his, and if you maintain a proper defense you'll manage a draw. That's the best you can hope for."

Once more we were astounded. There was something bewildering about both the precision and the speed of his calculations; it was as though he saw the moves printed in a book. In any event, his intervention and the unanticipated opportunity to draw against a world champion had a magical effect. We moved aside as one to give him a clearer view of the board. Again McConnor asked:

"So, king g8 to h7?"

"Right! The main thing is to keep in the clear!"

McConnor did as he was told, and we tapped on the glass. Czentovic strode over to our table with his usual composure and assessed our move with one glance. He then moved his king's pawn h2–h4—exactly as predicted by our unknown collaborator, who was already whispering excitedly:

"Advance the rook, advance the rook, c8 to c4, then he'll have to cover his pawn first. But that won't help him! You'll capture it with your knight d3–e5, no need to worry about his free pawn, and you'll be on an even footing again. Press the attack, stop defending!"

We did not understand this. It was Greek to us. But McConnor was under his spell, and again obeyed automatically. We tapped on the glass once more to summon Czentovic. For the first time he did not decide quickly, but studied the board with furrowed brow. He then made precisely the move fore-told by the stranger and turned to go. But before he walked away, something new and unexpected happened. Czentovic raised his eyes and reviewed our ranks; he evidently wished to discover who was suddenly putting up such energetic resistance.

From that moment on, our excitement grew beyond measure. Until then we had played without any serious hope, but now the idea of breaking Czentovic's cold arrogance quickened all our pulses. Our new friend had already indicated the next move, and we were ready to summon Czentovic—my fingers trembled as I struck the glass with the spoon. And now came our first triumph. Czentovic, who until then had always played on his feet, hesitated, hesitated, and finally sat down. He sat down slowly and ponderously; but with this movement alone the former *de haut en bas* inequality between us had been abolished. We had brought him down to our level, at least in a physical sense. He thought a long time, his eyes fixed on the board and downcast so that his pupils were hardly visible under the shadowed lids, and as he did his mouth gradually fell open, giving his round face a somewhat simple-minded appearance. Czentovic meditated intensely for some minutes, then made his move and rose. And already our friend was whispering:

"He's stalling! Good thinking! But pay no attention! Force an exchange, an exchange at all costs, then we can draw, and not even God can help him."

McConnor did as he was told. The next few moves were an incomprehensible give-and-take between the two antagonists (the rest of us had long since become mere supernumeraries). Some seven moves later, Czentovic looked up after long thought and said, "Draw."

For a moment there was complete silence. You could suddenly hear the murmur of the waves, the jazz from the radio in the lounge, every footstep from the promenade deck, and the faint, delicate whistling of the wind through the cracks in the windows. Nobody breathed, it had happened too suddenly, and all of us were still almost in a state of shock after this improbable occurrence—this stranger had imposed his will on the world champion in a game that was half lost. McConnor leaned back suddenly, and the breath he had been holding escaped from his lips with a delighted "Ah!" I then observed Czentovic. During the last few moves it seemed to me that he had become paler. But he had no difficulty in maintaining his self-possession. He kept up a serene front and merely asked in the most unconcerned way, as he smoothly pushed the pieces off the board:

"Do the gentlemen wish a third game?"

He asked the question in a purely professional, businesslike manner. But this was the remarkable thing: instead of looking at McConnor, he had sharply and directly raised his eyes to our benefactor. During the last moves he must have recognized his real, his true opponent just as a horse knows a new, better rider by the way he takes the saddle. Involuntarily we followed his gaze, looking eagerly at the stranger. But before he had a chance to consider, much less respond, McConnor, bursting with pride and excitement, had called out triumphantly:

"Of course! But now you have to play Czentovic by yourself! Just you against Czentovic!"

But now something unforeseen happened. The stranger, who rather oddly was still staring intently at the empty chessboard, gave a start, feeling all eyes upon him and hearing himself addressed with such enthusiasm. He looked confused.

"Impossible, gentlemen," he stammered, visibly disconcerted. "It's completely out of the question... You shouldn't even consider me...It's been twenty, no, twenty-five years since I sat down at a chessboard...and only now do I see my impertinence in meddling in your game without being asked... Please excuse me for being so presumptuous...I certainly won't bother you again." And before we could recover from our surprise, he had already walked away and left the room.

"But this is incredible!" boomed the temperamental McConnor, banging his fist on the table. "It can't be twenty-five years since this man played chess! He was calculating every move, every response five, six moves ahead. Nobody can do that off the top of his head. That's completely impossible—isn't it?"

As he asked this last question McConnor had turned without thinking to Czentovic. But the world champion remained unflappable.

"I am unable to say. However, the gentleman's game was somewhat surprising and interesting; that is why I deliberately gave him a chance." Rising nonchalantly, he added in his professional manner:

"If the gentleman, or you gentlemen, should wish another game tomorrow, I shall be at your service from three o'clock on."

We could not suppress a faint smile. As we all knew, Czentovic had certainly not magnanimously given our unknown benefactor a chance, and this remark was nothing more than a simple-minded excuse for his own failure. Our desire to see such imperturbable arrogance brought low grew all the more fiercely. Peaceable, idle passengers though we were, we had suddenly been seized by a wild, ambitious bellicosity, tantalized and aroused by the thought that the palm might be wrested from the champion right here on this ship in the middle of the ocean, a feat that would then be telegraphed around the globe. There was also the allure of mystery, the effect of our benefactor's unexpected intervention just at the critical moment, and the contrast between his almost anxious diffidence and the imperturbable self-assurance of the professional. Who was this stranger? Had chance brought to light an as yet undiscovered chess genius? Or was he a renowned master who was concealing his identity from us for some unfathomable reason? We debated all these possibilities in a state of utmost excitement; even the most daring hypotheses were not daring enough for us to square the stranger's puzzling timidity and surprising avowal with the unmistakable artfulness of his play. But on one point we were agreed: on no account would we forgo the spectacle of a return engagement. We resolved to do everything to have our benefactor play against Czentovic the next day; McConnor agreed to bear the financial risk. In the meantime it had been learned from the steward that the stranger was an Austrian. Thus it fell to me, as his compatriot, to convey our request.

I soon found the man who had fled so hurriedly. He was on the promenade deck, reading in a deck chair. Before presenting myself I took the opportunity to study him. The angular head rested in an attitude of mild fatigue on the cushion; I was again especially struck by the remarkable pallor of the comparatively young face, framed at the temples by blindingly white hair. I had the feeling, I don't know why, that this man must have aged abruptly. I had hardly approached him when he rose politely and introduced himself, using a name which was immediately familiar to me as that of a highly regarded old Austrian family. I recalled that one of the bearers of this name had been part of Schubert's most intimate circle and that one of the old Kaiser's personal physicians had descended from the same family. When I conveyed to Dr. B. our request that he accept Czentovic's challenge, he was visibly astonished. As it turned out, he had had no idea that it was a world champion, in fact the reigning one, against whom he had so magnificently held his own in that game. For some reason this information seemed to make a special impression on him, for he asked over and over if I was sure his opponent really was the acknowledged world champion. I soon found that this state of affairs made my task easier and, aware of his sensitivity, considered it advisable to conceal from him only that the financial risk of possible defeat was being borne by McConnor. After hesitating for quite a while, Dr. B. finally declared himself ready for a match, though not without expressly asking me to warn the other gentlemen that it was imperative not to place exaggerated hopes in his abilities.

"You see," he added with a pensive smile, "I honestly don't know if I can play a proper chess game according to all the rules. Please believe me, it was absolutely not out of false modesty that I said I hadn't touched a chess piece since grammar school—that was more than twenty years ago. And even then I wasn't considered a player of any particular talent."

He said this so naturally that it was impossible to entertain the least doubt as to his sincerity. Nevertheless, I could not help but express my astonishment at the precision with which he had been able to remember every combination of moves played by a variety of chess masters; surely he must have been much involved with chess theory, at least? Dr. B. smiled once again in that oddly dreamy way.

"Much involved!—God knows you'd have to say I was much involved with chess. But it happened under quite special, indeed entirely unique circumstances. It's a fairly complicated story, and one that might possibly be considered a small contribution to the delightful, grand times we live in. If you will bear with me for half an hour..."

He had motioned toward the deck chair next to him. I gladly accepted his invitation. We had no neighbors. Dr. B. removed his reading glasses, put them aside, and began:

"You were good enough to mention that you remembered my family name, since you are from Vienna yourself. But I hardly think you will have heard of the legal firm which I directed with my father and later on by myself, for we didn't take cases you might have read about in the papers and deliberately avoided new clients. The truth is that we didn't have a proper legal practice, but limited ourselves to legal consulting for the large monasteries with which my father, formerly a representative of the clerical party, was closely associated, and especially to administering their estates. We were also entrusted with managing the finances of certain members of the imperial family (I'm sure it's all right to talk about this, now that the monarchy has passed into history). These connections with the court and the clergy—an uncle of mine was the Kaiser's personal physician, another an abbot in Seitenstetten—went back two generations; we had only to keep them up, and it was a quiet, you could even say 'silent' employment that was granted us through this inherited commission, requiring little more than the strictest discretion and dependability, two traits which my late father possessed in the highest degree; in fact his prudence enabled him to preserve the considerable fortunes of his clients during the years of the inflation and the economic collapse that followed. Then when Hitler took the helm in Germany and began his raids on the property of the Church and the monasteries, we handled a variety of negotiations and transactions (some of them even originating abroad) to save at least the movable assets from being impounded. The two of us knew more about certain secret political negotiations of the Curia and the imperial family than the public will ever learn of. But the very inconspicuousness of our office (we didn't even have a sign on the door), as well as the care with which we both pointedly avoided monarchist circles, provided the safest protection from unwanted inquiries. During all those years, in fact, none of the Austrian authorities ever suspected that secret couriers were collecting and depositing the imperial family's most important mail right at our modest office on the fourth floor.

"Now the Nazis, long before they built up their armies against the world, had begun to organize an equally dangerous and well-trained army in all neighboring countries—the legion of the disadvantaged, the neglected, the aggrieved. Their 'cells' were tucked away in every office, every business; their informers and spies were everywhere, all the way up to the private chambers of Dollfuss and Schuschnigg. They had their man even in our obscure office, as I unfortunately failed to discover until it was too late. He was admittedly no more than a miserable, useless clerk, whom I had only hired on the recommendation of a vicar in order to give the office the outward appearance of an ordinary business; in fact we used him for nothing but innocent errands, had him answer the telephone and file papers—completely insignificant and harmless ones, that is. He was never allowed to open the mail, I typed all the important correspondence myself without making copies, I took any essential documents home and shifted all confidential meetings to the priory of the monastery or my uncle's surgery. Thanks to these precautions, the informer learned nothing vital; but some unfortunate accident must have told the vain and ambitious fellow that he was not trusted and that all sorts of interesting things were going on behind his back. Perhaps in my absence one of the couriers had carelessly spoken of 'His Majesty' instead of (as agreed) 'Baron Fern,' or the scoundrel disobeyed his instructions and opened some letters—in any event, he got orders from Berlin or Munich to keep an eye on us before I had time to become suspicious. Only much later, when I had been incarcerated for a long time, did I remember that his initial laziness at work had turned into sudden zeal during the last months and that on repeated occasions he had practically insisted on mailing my correspondence. So I cannot absolve myself of a certain carelessness. But, after all, didn't Hitler and his bunch insidiously outmaneuver even the greatest diplomats and military men? Just how closely and lovingly the Gestapo had been watching over me for all that time became blatantly clear when I was arrested by the SS on the very evening that Schuschnigg announced his abdication, one day before Hitler marched into Vienna. Luckily I had been able to burn the most critical papers as soon as I heard Schuschnigg's farewell speech on the radio, and (really at the last minute, before those fellows beat my door down) I sent the rest of the documents, including the all-important records of the assets held abroad for the monasteries and two archdukes, over to my uncle, carried hidden in a laundry basket by my trusty old housekeeper."

Dr. B. paused to light a cigar. In the flare of light I noticed a nervous twitching at the right corner of his mouth, something that had struck me earlier. I saw now that it was repeated every few minutes. The movement was a fleeting one, hardly more than a flicker, but it gave his entire face a peculiar restlessness.

"You're probably thinking that now I'm going to tell you about the concentration camp where all those loyal to our old Austria were taken, about the

humiliations, torments, ordeals I suffered there. But
nothing of the kind occurred. I was in another category. I was not made to join those unfortunates upon
whom the Nazis vented their long-harbored resent-
ments by inflicting physical and spiritual degrada-
tions; I was placed in that other, rather small group
of people from whom the Nazis hoped to extract either money or important information. An insignificant person like me was of course of no interest to
the Gestapo for my own sake. However, they must
have learned that we were the front men, the trustees
and intimates of their bitterest enemies, and must
have hoped to extort some incriminating evidence:
evidence against the monasteries proving illicit re-
moval of assets, evidence against the imperial family
and all those in Austria who were selflessly fighting
for the monarchy. They suspected—in truth, not
without good reason—that substantial reserves of the
assets which had passed through our hands were still
hidden away where they couldn't steal them; they
brought me in on the very first day to force these secrets out of me using their time-tested methods.
People in my category, from whom important evidence or money was to be extracted, were therefore
not stowed in concentration camps, but saved for
special treatment. You will perhaps remember that
our chancellor, and in a different sort of case Baron

Rothschild, from whose relatives they hoped to wring millions, were not put behind barbed wire in a prison camp. By no means. Instead, as if they were being accorded preferential treatment, they were taken to a hotel, the Hotel Metropole—also the Gestapo's headquarters—where they were each given separate rooms. Insignificant as I may have been, I was also granted this distinction.

"My own room in a hotel—that sounds awfully decent, doesn't it? Believe me, though, if they housed 'celebrities' like us in reasonably well-heated hotel rooms of our own, this was not intended to be more decent than cramming us by the score into an ice-cold barracks—it was just a subtler method. For the requisite 'evidence' was to be wrested from us by a force more sophisticated than crude beating or physical torture: the most exquisite isolation imaginable. They did nothing—other than subjecting us to complete nothingness. For, as is well known, nothing on earth puts more pressure on the human mind than nothing. Locking each of us into a total vacuum, a room hermetically sealed off from the outside world, instead of beating us or exposing us to cold—this was meant to create an internal pressure that would finally force our lips open. At first glance the room assigned to me did not seem at all uncomfortable. It had a door, a bed, a chair, a washbasin, a barred window. But the door stayed locked day and night, no book, no newspaper, no sheet of paper or pencil was permitted to be on the table, the window faced a firewall; complete nothingness surrounded me both physically and psychologically. They had taken every object away from me—I had no watch, so that I didn't know the time; no pencil, so that I couldn't write; no knife, so that I couldn't slit my wrists; even the tiniest comfort, such as a cigarette, was denied me. Apart from the guard, who was not permitted to say a word or respond to questions, I never saw a human face, never heard a human voice; my eyes, my ears, all my senses received not the slightest stimulation from morning till night, from night till morning, all the time you were hopelessly alone with yourself, with your body, and with these four or five mute objects, table, bed, window, washbasin; you lived like a diver in a diving bell in the black sea of this silence, for that matter like a diver who has guessed that the cable to the outside world has snapped and that he will never be hauled out of the silent deep. There was nothing to do, nothing to hear, nothing to see, nothingness was everywhere around me all the time, a completely dimensionless and timeless void. You walked up and down, you and your thoughts, up and down, over and over. But even thoughts, insubstantial as they seem, need a footing, or they begin to spin, to run in frenzied circles; they can't bear noth-ingness either. You waited for something from morn-ing until night, and nothing happened. You went on waiting and waiting. Nothing happened. You waited, waited, waited, thinking, thinking, thinking, until your temples throbbed. Nothing happened. You were alone. Alone. Alone.

"This went on for fourteen days, during which I lived outside time, outside the world. If a war had broken out then, I wouldn't have known it; my world was nothing more than desk, door, bed, washbasin, chair, window, and wall, I stared always at the same wallpaper on the same wall; every line of its jagged pattern became etched as though by a burin into the innermost recesses of my brain, that's how much I stared at it. Then finally the interrogations began. You were suddenly sent for, not knowing if it was day or night. They summoned you and led you, not knowing where you were going, down a few passage-ways; then you waited somewhere, not knowing where, and suddenly you were standing in front of a table, around which sat several uniformed men. On the table was a stack of paper, the files whose con-tents were unknowable, and then the questions started—the real ones and the fake ones, the straight-forward ones and the malicious ones, sham ques-tions, trick questions—and while you answered, a stranger's cruel fingers were shuffling through papers whose contents were unknowable and a stranger's cruel fingers were writing something unknowable in a report. But for me the most terrible thing about these interrogations was that I could never divine or figure out what the Gestapo actually knew about what went on in my office and what they were just trying to get out of me now. As I mentioned before, at the eleventh hour I had sent the really incriminating papers to my uncle in the care of the housekeeper. But had he received them? Or had he not? And how much had that clerk given away? How many letters had they intercepted, how much had they learned by now in the German monasteries which we represented, perhaps squeezed out of some unfortunate churchman? And the questions kept coming. What securities had I bought for a certain monastery, what banks did I correspond with, did I know a Mr. So-and-So, had I received letters from Switzerland or East Nowhere. And since I could never tell how much they had already ferreted out, every statement became the most terrible responsibility. If I gave away something they didn't know, I might be delivering someone to the knife unnecessarily. If I denied too much, I was hurting myself.

"But the interrogation wasn't the worst part. The worst part was coming back after the interrogation to my nothingness, the same room with the same table, the same bed, the same washbasin, the same wallpaper. For as soon as I was by myself I tried to formulate what I should have said if I had been smarter and what I should say next time to allay any suspicion I might have aroused by a thoughtless remark. I mulled over, pondered, examined, scrutinized every word I had said to the interrogator, I recapitulated every question they asked, every answer I gave, I tried to decide what they might have chosen to write down, though I knew I could never reach a conclusion and could never find out. But these thoughts, once set in motion in the empty room, did not stop revolving in my head, always fresh, in ever new permutations—they even invaded my sleep; after every interrogation by the Gestapo my own thoughts relentlessly continued the torment of questioning and examining and harassing—even more cruelly, perhaps, for the former came to an end after an hour but the latter never did, thanks to the insidious torture of this solitude. And all the time nothing around me but the table, the bureau, the bed, the wallpaper, the window, no distraction, no book, no newspaper, no new face, no pencil to write anything down with, no matches to play with, nothing, nothing, nothing. Now I saw how diabolically practical, how psychologically deadly in its conception this hotel room system was. In a concentration camp you might have had to cart stones around until your hands bled and your feet froze in your shoes, you would have been jammed together with two dozen other men in the cold and stench. But you would have seen faces, you would have been able to look at a field, a cart, a tree, a star, something, anything, whereas here it was always the same thing around you, always the same thing, the terrible sameness. Here there was nothing to distract me from my thoughts, from my delusions, from my morbid rehearsals of past events. And that was exactly what they wanted—that I should go on gagging on my thoughts until I choked on them and had no choice but to spit them out, to inform, to tell everything, to finally hand over the evidence and the people they wanted. Little by little I sensed how my nerves were beginning to give under the dreadful pressure of nothingness, and, aware of the danger, I strained myself to the breaking point to find or invent some diversion. To occupy my mind I tried to reconstruct and recite everything I had ever learned by heart, the anthems and nursery rhymes of childhood, the Homer I'd learned in grade school, the sections of the Civil Code. Then I tried arithmetic—adding and dividing random figures—but nothing stuck in my mind in that emptiness. I couldn't concentrate on anything. The same flickering thought always broke in: What do they know? What did I say yesterday, what must I say next time?

"This truly indescribable state of affairs continued for four months. Now four months is easy to write: so many letters, no more, no less! It's easy to say: four months—two syllables. It takes no time at all to form the words: four months! But there's no way to describe, to gauge, to delineate, not for someone else, not for yourself, how long time lasts in dimensionlessness, in timelessness, and you can't explain to anyone how it eats at you and destroys you, this nothing and nothing and nothing around you, always this table and bed and washbasin and wallpaper, and always the silence, always the same guard pushing food in without looking at you, always the same thoughts in that nothingness revolving around a single thought, until you go mad. Little things made me uncomfortably aware that my mind was falling into disorder. At the beginning I had still been lucid during the interrogations, my statements had been calm and considered; that duality of thought by which I knew what to say and what not to say was still functioning. Now I stammered when I tried to get out even the simplest sentences, for while I spoke I stared, hypnotized, at the pen that ran across the paper taking down what I said, as though I wanted to chase after my own words. I sensed that my strength was failing,

I sensed that the moment was approaching when, to save myself, I would tell everything I knew, and perhaps more, when I would betray twelve people and their secrets to escape the chokehold of this nothingness, without gaining anything more than a moment's rest for myself. One evening it had come to this: when the guard happened to bring me my food in this moment of suffocation, I suddenly shouted after him, 'Take me to the interrogation! I'll tell everything! I want to make a full statement! I'll say where the papers are, where the money is! I'll tell everything, everything!' Luckily he didn't hear me. Perhaps he didn't want to hear me.

"At this moment of greatest need, something unforeseen happened that promised to save me, at least for a time. It was the end of July, a dark, overcast, rainy day: I remember this detail clearly because the rain was hammering against the windowpanes in the corridor through which I was led to the interrogation. I had to wait in an anteroom. You always had to wait to be brought before the interrogator: having you wait was another part of the technique. First they shattered your nerves when they summoned you, suddenly pulling you out of your cell in the middle of the night, and then, when you had prepared yourself for the interrogation, when your mind and will were steeled, they made you wait, pointlessly and pointedly, for one hour, two hours, three hours before the interrogation, to exhaust you physically and wear you down mentally. And they made me wait a particularly long time on this Wednesday, the 27th of July, two whole hours on my feet in the anteroom; I remember this fact too for a particular reason: in this anteroom, where I had to stand for two hours until I was ready to drop (I wasn't permitted to sit down, of course), hung a calendar, and I am not capable of explaining to you how, in my hunger for anything printed, anything written, I stared and stared at that one number, that little bit of writing 'July 27' on the wall; my brain devoured it, you could say. Then I went on waiting and waiting and stared at the door, wondering when it would finally open and what the inquisitors might ask this time, though I knew that what they asked would be quite different from anything I was preparing for. Yet in spite of everything the agony of this waiting and standing was at the same time a relief, a pleasure, because this room was at least different from mine, somewhat larger and with two windows instead of one, without the bed and without the washbasin and without that particular crack in the windowsill that I had looked at a million times. The door was painted a different color, there was a different chair against the wall and to the left of it a file cabinet with files and a coatrack with hangers on which three or four damp military coats were hanging, the coats of my tormentors. So I had something fresh, something different to look at with my ravenous eyes, something new at last, and they clutched avidly at every detail. I examined every crease in those coats, I noticed for example a raindrop hanging from one of the wet collars, and, as ridiculous as it may sound to you, I waited with absurd excitement to see whether this drop would eventually run off along the crease, or whether it would defy gravity and keep clinging—yes, I stared and stared at that drop breathlessly for minutes on end as though my life depended on it. Then, when it had finally rolled off, I counted the buttons on the coats over again, eight on one, eight on another, ten on the third, and compared the lapels once more; my voracious eyes touched, caressed, embraced all these ridiculous, trivial details with a hunger I am unable to describe. And suddenly my gaze was riveted on something. I had discovered a slight bulge in the side pocket of one of the coats. I moved closer and thought I knew from the rectangular shape of the bulge what was in this slightly swollen pocket: a book! My knees began to shake: a BOOK! For four months I had not held a book in my hands, and there was something intoxicating and at the same time stupefying in the mere thought of a book, in which you could see words one after another, lines, paragraphs, pages, a book in which you could read, follow, take into your mind the new, different, diverting thoughts of another person. Mesmerized, I stared at the little convexity of the book in the pocket, they blazed at that one inconspicuous spot as though they wanted to burn a hole in the coat. Finally I could not control my craving; without thinking I moved closer. The mere thought that I might so much as feel a book through the material made my fingers tingle down to the tips. Almost without knowing it, I crept closer. Fortunately the guard paid no attention to my behavior, though it was undoubtedly odd; perhaps it seemed only natural to him that someone who had been on his feet for two hours might want to lean against the wall for a moment. Finally I was standing right next to the coat; I had carefully put my hands behind my back so I could touch it without attracting attention. I touched the cloth and sure enough felt something rectilinear through it, something that was flexible and rustled slightly—a book! A book! And the idea flashed through my mind like a bullet: steal this book! Maybe you'll succeed, you can hide it in your cell and then read, read, read, finally read again! Once this idea had entered my head, it was like a strong poison; my ears began to ring and my heart began to pound, my hands became ice-cold and paralyzed. But after a dazed moment I gently, stealthily pressed still closer to the coat; with my hands hidden behind my back, I nudged the book from the bottom of the pocket, higher and higher, my eye on the guard all the while. And then I grasped it; one gentle, careful tug, and the book, small, not too thick, was in my hand. Now that I had done the deed, I was frightened for the first time. But there was no going back. Yet where could I put it? Behind my back I pushed the volume inside the waistband of my trousers and from there, bit by bit, over to my hip, so that as I walked I could hold on to it with my hand pressed military-style to the seam in my trousers. Now came the first test. I walked away from the coatrack, one step, two steps, three steps. It worked. If I kept my hand pressed firmly to my belt, it was possible to walk and at the same time hold the book fast.

"Then came the interrogation. It took more effort on my part than ever, for when I answered I was actually concentrating with all my power not on what I was saying but first and foremost on keeping hold of the book without attracting attention. Fortunately the interrogation was brief this time, and I carried the book safely to my room—I won't trouble you with all the details; there was a dangerous moment when it slipped down out of my trousers in the middle of the corridor and I had to simulate a severe fit of coughing in order to bend down and push it safely under my belt again. But on the other hand what a moment it was when, still carrying the book, I stepped back into my hell, alone at last and yet no longer alone!

"Now you'll probably think that I immediately seized the book, examined it, and read it. Not at all! First I wanted to savor to the full the anticipatory pleasure of having a book, the artificially prolonged delight, with a wonderful arousing effect on my nerves, of imagining the stolen book in detail, imagining what sort of book I'd most like it to be: closely printed above all, with many, many characters, many, many thin pages, so there would be more to read. And then I wanted it to be a work that required intellectual effort, nothing shallow, nothing easy, but something you could study, learn by heart, poems, and preferably—I had the audacity to dream of such a thing—Goethe or Homer. But finally I could no longer control my eagerness, my curiosity. Stretched out on the bed, so that the guard wouldn't catch me by surprise if he suddenly opened the door, I tremblingly brought out the volume from under my belt.

"When I saw the book, my first reaction was disappointment, even a kind of bitter anger: this book, captured at such atrocious risk and safeguarded with such ardent expectation, was nothing more or less than a sourcebook for chess players, an anthology of a hundred fifty master games. If I hadn't been behind bars I would have hurled it through an open window in fury, for what was I supposed to do, what could I do with this nonsense? Like most schoolboys, I had occasionally been driven by boredom to give chess a try. But what good was this theoretical rubbish? You can't play chess without another player and certainly not without pieces, without a board. Morosely I turned the pages, hoping I might still find something readable, a preface, some instruction; but I found nothing but plain square diagrams of each of the master games and underneath them symbols that were incomprehensible to me at first, a2–a3, Nf1–g3, and so on. It all seemed to me like a kind of mathematical code, to which I lacked the key. I only gradually deciphered it: to designate the positions of the pieces, the letters a, b, c, etc. stood for the vertical rows and the numerals 1 through 8 for the horizontal rows; so that these diagrams, though schematic, had a language all the same. Perhaps, I thought, I could construct a kind of chessboard in my cell and then try to play these games through; like a sign from heaven it came to me that my bedspread happened to have a large checkered pattern. If you folded it properly, you could eventually produce an arrangement of sixty-four squares. So the first thing I did was to hide the book under the mattress, having torn out the first page. Then I began to fashion chess pieces, the king, the queen, and so on, out of crumbs of bread I had saved; the results were of course absurdly crude, but, after interminable effort, I was finally able to set about reconstructing on the checkered bedspread the positions depicted in the book. But when I tried to play through an entire game with my ridiculous crumb chessmen, half of which I had darkened with dust to set them apart from the others, at first I failed totally. During those early days I was constantly becoming confused; I had to start this one game from the beginning over and over again—five times, ten times, twenty times. But who under the sun had so much unoccupied and unoccupiable time as I, the slave of nothingness? Who had such infinite reserves of desire and patience? After six days I played the game perfectly all the way through; after another eight days I didn't even need the crumbs on the bedspread to make the positions in the book real to me; and after eight more days I could do without the checkered bedspread—the symbols in the book, a1, a2, c7, c8, which had been abstract at the beginning, automatically turned into visible, three-dimensional positions in my head. The transformation was total: I had created an internal projection of the chessboard and pieces and was able to see any position based on nothing more than the formulas in the book, the way an expert musician has only to glance at a score to hear all the voices and their harmonization. After another fourteen days I was able to play through every game in the book effortlessly and by heart—I played 'blind,' to use the technical term; only now was I beginning to understand what an immeasurable boon my brazen theft had gained for me. For suddenly I had something to do—something meaningless, something without purpose, you may say, but still something that nullified the nullity surrounding me; I possessed in these one hundred fifty tournament games a marvelous weapon against the oppressive monotony of my environs and my existence. To keep this new activity exciting, I began to map out my day precisely: two games in the morning, two games in the afternoon, then a quick recap in the evening. So my day, otherwise as formless as jelly, was full, I was busy, without becoming tired, for chess had the marvelous merit that, because the intellectual energies were corralled within a narrowly circumscribed field, even the most strenuous mental effort did not tire the brain, but rather increased its agility and vigor. At first I played the games through quite mechanically; yet gradually a pleasurable, aesthetic understanding awoke within me. I grasped the fine points, the perils and rigors of attack and defense, the technique of thinking ahead, planning moves and countermoves, and soon I was able to recognize the personality and style of each of the chess masters as unmistakably as one knows a poet from only a few of his lines; what had begun as no more than a way to pass the time was becoming a pleasure, and the figures of the great chess strategists—Alekhine, Lasker, Bogoljubov, Tartakower, and the rest—became beloved companions in my solitude. Each day my silent cell was filled with ceaseless novelty, and the very regularity of my *exercitia* restored the acuity of my intellectual faculties: I felt my mind refreshed, even honed, so to speak, by the constant mental discipline. The fact that I was thinking more clearly and coherently was especially evident during the interrogations. At the chessboard I had unconsciously perfected a defense against false threats and concealed tricks; from then on I no longer let down my guard during the questioning, and it even seemed to me that the Gestapo men were beginning to regard me with a certain respect. They had seen all the others break; perhaps they were quietly wondering what secret wellspring had given me alone the strength for such unshakable resistance.

"This happy time continued for about two and a half or three months: day after day I systematically played through the hundred fifty games in that book. Then, unexpectedly, I came to a standstill. Suddenly I was once again facing nothingness. For once I had played each game twenty or thirty times through, it lost the charm of novelty, of surprise, its previous power to excite, to arouse, was exhausted. What was the point of repeating over and over games whose every move I had long since learned by heart? As soon as I made the opening move, the succeeding ones automatically reeled off in my mind, there was nothing unanticipated, no suspense, no problems to solve. To keep myself busy, to create the demands and the distraction that I now couldn't do without, I would actually have needed another book with different games. But since this was completely impossible, there was only one way to continue with this strange diversion: I had to make up new games to replace the old ones. I had to try to play with, or rather against, myself.

"Now I don't know how much thought you have given to what goes on intellectually in this most remarkable of games. But a moment's reflection should be enough to tell you that in chess, a game of pure reasoning with no element of chance, it is a logical absurdity to want to play oneself. The basic attraction of chess lies solely in the fact that its strategy is worked out differently in two different minds, that in this battle of wits Black does not know White's schemes and constantly seeks to guess them and frustrate them, while White in turn tries to outstrip and thwart Black's secret intentions. Now if Black and White together made up one and the same person, the result would be a nonsensical state of affairs in which one and the same mind simultaneously knew and did not know something, in which as White it could simply decide to forget what it had wished and intended to do as Black a moment earlier. In fact what is presupposed by this kind of duality of thought is a total division of consciousness, an ability to turn the workings of the brain on or off at will, as though it were a machine; playing chess against oneself is thus as paradoxical as jumping over one's own shadow. Well, to make a long story short, in my desperation I attempted this impossibility, this absurdity, for months. Illogical as it was, I had no other choice if I was not to lapse into absolute madness or total intellectual inanition. My awful situation was forcing me to at least try to divide myself into a Black Me and a White Me in order not to be crushed by the horrendous nothingness around me."

Dr. B. leaned back in his deck chair and closed his eyes for a moment. It was as though he was trying to forcibly repress a disturbing memory. Again there was the strange uncontrollable twitch at the left corner of his mouth. Then he drew himself up a little higher in his reclining chair.

"So—I hope I've been fairly clear so far. But unfortunately I'm not at all certain that I can make you see the rest of it as clearly. For this new occupation required such total mental exertion that it became impossible to keep a grip on myself at the same time. I said that I think it's inherently absurd to want to play chess against yourself; nevertheless, this absurdity would stand a minimal chance if you had a chessboard in front of you, because the board's reality would give it a certain distance, some outward substance. In front of a real chessboard with real pieces you can stop to think, you can physically position yourself first on one side of the table, then on the other, considering the situation first from Black's standpoint, then from White's. But obliged as I was to project this battle against myself (or with myself, if you like) within an imaginary space, I was forced to keep the current position on the sixty-four squares firmly in my mind's eye, and compute not just the present configuration, but also the possible later moves of both players, and even—I know how absurd it all sounds—to visualize them twice and three times, no, six times, eight times, twelve times, for each me, for Black and for White, four and five moves ahead. Playing in the abstract realm of the imagination, I had to (excuse me for putting you through this madness) compute four or five moves ahead both as Player White and as Player Black, that is, I had to think through the situations that might arise in the development of the game so to speak with two minds, my white mind and my black mind. But the most dangerous thing in my abstruse experiment was not even this self-division, but the fact that devising games on my own was suddenly causing me to lose my footing and fall into the abyss. Playing through the master games as I had done in previous weeks was ultimately no more than an effort of repetition, a mere recapitulation of existing material, and as such no more strenuous than learning poetry by heart or memorizing sections of the legal code; it was a limited, disciplined activity and for that reason an excellent mental exercise. The two games I ran through every morning and every afternoon represented a set pensum which I completed without becoming agitated; they took the place of a normal occupation, and, further, if I made a mistake in the course of a game or forgot how to go on, I always had the book. The only reason that this activity had become such a salutary and even soothing one for my shattered nerves was that playing through games that were not my own did not involve me personally; it was all the same to me whether Black or White won, it was Alekhine or Bogoljubov who was battling for the laurels of the champion, and I as a person, my intellect, my spirit took part solely as an observer, as a connoisseur of the peripeteias and the beauties of each game. But from the moment I began to play against myself, I began unwittingly to challenge myself. Each of my two selves, the black one and the white one, had to vie against the other, and each conceived its own ambition, its own impatience, to gain the ascendancy, to win; after each move as White, I was in a fever to know what Black would do. Each of the two selves exulted when the other made a mistake and became exasperated at its own bungling.

"All of this seems senseless, and in fact this kind of artificial schizophrenia or divided consciousness, with its admixture of dangerous excitation, would be inconceivable in a normal person under normal circumstances. But don't forget that I had been forcibly wrenched out of any sort of normal life, I was a prisoner, unjustly held in captivity, exquisitely tormented with solitude for months, I had long wanted something upon which to vent my accumulated fury. And since I had nothing but this nonsensical playing against myself, my fury, my desire for vengeance was fanatically channeled into this game. Something in me wanted to come out on top, and yet all there was

for me to fight was this other me in me; so as I
played I worked myself up into a state of almost
manic excitement. At the beginning my thinking was
calm and considered, I took breaks between one
game and the next in order to recover from my agitation; but gradually my frayed nerves refused to let me
wait. My white self had no sooner made a move than
my black self feverishly pushed forward; a game was
no sooner over than I challenged myself to another,
for one of the two chess selves was beaten by the
other every time and demanded a rematch. I couldn't
even begin to say how many games this mad insatia-
bility made me play against myself during these last
months—a thousand, perhaps, maybe more. It was
an obsession which I could not resist; from morning
till night I thought of nothing but bishop and pawns
and rook and king and a and b and c and mate and
castling; my entire being and all my feeling were im-
mersed in the checkered board. My pleasure in playing became a desire to play, the desire to play became
a compulsion to play, a mania, a frenzy, which per-
meated not only my waking hours but gradually my
sleep too. Chess was all I could think about, chess
moves, chess problems were the only form my
thoughts could take; sometimes I awoke with a
sweaty brow and understood that I must have unconsciously gone on playing even while I slept, and if

I dreamt of people, all they did was move like the bishop or the rook, or hopscotch like the knight. Even when I was summoned to an interrogation, I could no longer think coherently about my responsibilities; I have a feeling that during the final interrogations I must have expressed myself pretty confusedly, for the interrogators looked at each other with surprise. But while they asked questions and consulted with one another, all I was waiting for in my wretched craving was to be taken back to my cell so that I could go on with my playing, my insane playing, a new game and then another and another. Any interruption disturbed me; even the quarter of an hour while the guard cleaned the cell, the two minutes when he brought me my food, was a torment to me in my feverish impatience; sometimes the bowl containing my meal was still untouched in the evening; wrapped up in my playing, I had forgotten to eat. My only physical sensation was a terrible thirst; it must have been the fever of this constant thinking and playing; I drained the bottle in two gulps and pestered the guard for more, and yet my tongue was dry in my mouth a moment later. Finally my excitement while playing—and I did nothing else from morning till night—reached such a pitch that I could no longer sit still for a second; I walked up and down constantly while I thought about the games, faster and faster and faster, up and down, up and down, and more and more excitedly as a game's critical point approached; my eagerness to win, to dominate, to beat myself, gradually became a kind of frenzy, I trembled with impatience, for one chess-self always found the other too slow. One urged the other on; as ridiculous as it may seem to you, I began to berate myself—'Faster, faster!' or 'Go on, go on!'—when one me wasn't quick enough with a countermove. Today, of course, it's entirely clear to me that this state of mine was a thoroughly pathological form of mental overstimulation, for which I have found no name but one heretofore unknown to medicine: chess sickness. Ultimately this monomaniacal obsession began to attack my body as well as my mind. I lost weight, my sleep was troubled and fitful, when I woke up it always took special effort to force my leaden eyelids open; sometimes I felt so weak that when I held a glass it was all I could do to bring it to my lips, my hands were trembling so much; but as soon as I began to play, a furious energy came over me: I walked up and down with fists clenched, and I sometimes heard, as though through a red fog, my own voice addressing me with hoarse and ill-tempered exclamations of 'Check!' or 'Mate!'

"I myself am unable to tell you how this appalling, indescribable state came to a head. All I know is that

I woke up one morning and my awakening was not the same as usual. My body was as if detached from me, I was resting easily and comfortably. A dense, agreeable tiredness such as I had not known for months lay upon my eyelids, lay upon them with such warmth and beneficence that at first I could not bring myself to open my eyes. I was awake, but for minutes I enjoyed this heavy muzziness, the torpor of lying there with senses voluptuously dulled. Suddenly I seemed to hear voices behind me, living human voices speaking words, and you cannot imagine my joy, for it had been months, almost a year since I had heard words other than the harsh, cutting, malignant ones of my questioners. 'You're dreaming,' I said to myself. 'You're dreaming! Whatever you do, don't open your eyes! Let it go on, this dream, or you'll see that accursed room around you again, the chair and the washstand and the table and the wallpaper with the pattern always the same. You're dreaming—go on dreaming!'

"But curiosity got the better of me. Slowly and cautiously I opened my eyes. And, incredibly, it was a different room in which I found myself, a room wider and more spacious than my hotel room. An unbarred window let light in freely and looked out onto trees, green trees swaying in the breeze, instead of my unyielding firewall, the walls shone white and smooth, the ceiling above me was white and high—I really was in a new, different bed, and in fact it wasn't a dream, human voices were whispering softly behind me. I heard footsteps approaching, and I must have given an involuntary start of surprise. A woman glided up, a woman with a white cap over her hair, an attendant, a nurse. A shudder of joy passed over me: I hadn't seen a woman for a year. I stared at the sweet apparition, and it must have been a wild, ecstatic gaze, for the woman urgently soothed me: 'Be calm! Keep still!' But I only listened to her voice—wasn't that someone speaking? Was there really still someone on earth who wasn't an interrogator, a tormentor? And on top of that—what an incomprehensible miracle!—the soft, warm, almost tender voice of a woman. I stared greedily at her mouth, for in that year of hell it had come to seem unlikely to me that one person could speak kindly to another. She smiled at me—yes, she was smiling, there were still people who could smile kindly—then raised a finger of admonition to her lips and quietly moved away. But I could not do as she wished. I had not yet had enough of this miracle. I struggled to sit up in my bed in order to gaze after her, this miraculous human being who was kind. But when I tried to prop myself up on the edge of the bed, I couldn't. Where my right hand, my fingers and wrist, should have been, I felt something foreign, a big, fat, white ball, evidently a massive bandage. At first I gazed uncomprehendingly at this white, fat, foreign object on my hand; then I slowly began to understand where I was and to think about what might have happened to me. I must have been wounded, or I had injured my own hand. I was in a hospital.

"At midday the doctor came, a friendly older man. He knew my family name and spoke of my uncle, the Kaiser's personal physician, with such respect that I immediately felt he meant me well. As we went on he asked me all sorts of questions, particularly one that astonished me—whether I was a mathematician or a chemist. I said no.

"'Strange,' he murmured. 'While you were feverish you kept shouting out such strange formulas—c_3, c_4. None of us could make head or tail of it.'

"I asked what had happened to me. He smiled oddly.

"'Nothing serious. Acute nervous irritation,' he said, and added in low tones, after first looking around cautiously, 'Perfectly understandable when you get down to it. Since March 13, isn't that right?'

"I nodded.

"'No wonder, with these methods,' he murmured. 'You're not the first. But don't worry.'

"I knew from the comforting way he whispered

this to me and from the reassuring look on his face that I was in good hands.

"Two days later the kind doctor explained to me with some frankness what had happened. The guard had heard me cry out loudly in my cell and had at first thought I was quarreling with someone who had gotten in. But I had flung myself upon him the moment he appeared at the door and shouted wildly at him—things on the order of 'Will you make your move, you scoundrel, you coward!'—had tried to grab him by the throat, and finally assaulted him so fiercely that he had to call for help. When I was taken to be examined by a physician, in my derangement I had suddenly broken free, thrown myself at the window in the corridor and shattered the glass, cutting my hand—you can still see the deep scar here. I had spent my first few nights in the hospital with a kind of brain fever, but now the doctor said he found my sensorium entirely clear. 'Frankly,' he added quietly, 'I'd rather not tell the authorities, or eventually they'll take you back there again. Leave it to me, I'll do my best.'

"I have no idea what this helpful doctor told my tormentors about me. In any case he achieved what he had intended: my release. Possibly he declared me of unsound mind, or perhaps I had in the interval become unimportant to the Gestapo, for Hitler had now occupied Bohemia and the fall of Austria was thus over and done with as far as he was concerned. So I needed only to sign a commitment to leave the country within fourteen days. Those fourteen days were taken up with the hundred and one formalities that those who were once citizens of the world must now go through in order to travel abroad: military papers, police, tax, passport, visa, certificate of health. There was no time to think very much about what had happened. Whenever I did try to think back on my time in the cell, it was as though a light went out in my mind: apparently there are hidden regulatory forces at work within us which automatically shut off anything that might become psychologically trouble-some or dangerous. Only after weeks and weeks, really not until I was here aboard this ship, did I re-gain the courage to reflect on what had happened to me.

"And now you will understand my very imperti-nent and probably baffling behavior toward your friends. Quite by chance, I was strolling through the smoking lounge when I saw your friends sitting in front of the chessboard; I was rooted to the spot in stunned amazement. For I had completely forgotten that you can play chess at a real chessboard, with real pieces, forgotten that in this game two entirely differ-ent people can sit across from each other in the flesh.

It actually took me a few minutes to realize that what these players were engaged in was basically the same game that in desperation I had attempted to play against myself for months. The coded designations with which I had to make do during my grim *exercitia* were only stand-ins, symbolizing these ivory pieces; my surprise that this movement of pieces on the board was what I had visualized in subjective space could be compared to that of an astronomer who uses the most complex methods to work out on paper the existence of a new heavenly body and then actually sees it in the sky as a distinct, white, physical star. I stared at the board as though held by a magnet, seeing my figments, knight, rook, king, queen, and pawns, as real pieces carved out of wood; I had to transform my abstract computational world back into that of the pieces on the board before I could understand the state of play. Gradually I was overcome by curiosity to see a real game between two players. And then came the embarrassing moment when, forgetting all courtesy, I intruded on your game. But that bad move of your friend's hit a nerve. When I stopped him I was acting purely instinctively, I stepped in on impulse just as, without thinking, you seize a child who is leaning over a railing. My gross impertinence became clear to me only later."

I hastened to assure Dr. B. that we were all glad to

have had this unforeseen opportunity to make his acquaintance and that for me, after everything he had told me, it would be doubly interesting to be able to watch the improvised tournament the next day. Dr. B. shifted uneasily.

"No, really, don't expect too much. It will be nothing but a test for me...a test to see whether I... whether I am at all capable of playing an ordinary chess game, a game on a real chessboard with actual pieces and a live opponent...for now I doubt more and more whether those hundreds and perhaps thousands of games I played were actually proper chess games and not just a kind of dream chess, a fever chess, a delirium of play, skipping from one thing to another the way dreams do. I hope you will not seriously expect me to offer a genuine challenge to a chess master, indeed the greatest in the world. My only interest, the only attraction for me, is a postmortem curiosity to know whether that was chess or madness in the cell, whether at that time I was just on the brink or already over the edge—that's all, nothing else."

Just then the sound of a gong came from one end of the ship, summoning us to dinner. We must have been talking for two hours—Dr. B. reported everything in much more detail than I have set down here. I thanked him warmly and took my leave. But before

I could move along the deck, he came after me and, visibly nervous and even stammering a little, added:

"One more thing! Will you tell the gentlemen beforehand, so that I won't appear impolite afterwards: I'll play just one game...it's just to put paid to an old account—the finale rather than a new beginning...I don't want to fall again into that passionate chess fever, which I recall with nothing but horror ...and anyway...anyway the doctor warned me... warned me specifically. Anyone who has suffered from a mania remains at risk forever, and with chess sickness (even if cured) it would be better not to go near a chessboard...So you understand—only this one experimental game for myself, and no more."

The next day, we assembled in the smoking lounge punctually at the agreed-upon hour of three o'clock. Our group had grown to include two more lovers of the royal game, two ship's officers who had requested leave from duty so that they could watch the tournament. Even Czentovic did not keep us waiting as he had the previous day, and after the obligatory choice of colors the memorable game between this *homo obscurissimus* and the renowned world champion began. I regret that it was played for such thoroughly incompetent spectators and that its course is as lost to the annals of chess as Beethoven's piano improvisations are to music. On the succeeding afternoons we put our heads together to try to reconstruct the game from memory, but without success; we had probably been too intent on the two players to follow the progress of play. For the contrast in the two players' intellectual constitutions became more and more physically evident as the game proceeded. Czentovic, the old hand, remained stock-still the whole time, looking fixedly and severely down at the board: for him thought seemed to be close to physical exertion, demanding the utmost concentration in every part of his body. Dr. B. on the other hand moved completely freely and naturally. As a true dilettante in the best sense of the word, one who plays for the pure delight —that is, the *diletto*—of playing, he was utterly relaxed physically, chatting with us during the early breaks to explain the course of the game and casually lighting a cigarette. When it was his move he only glanced at the board. Each time he seemed to have been expecting his opponent's play.

The requisite opening moves went fairly quickly. Something like distinct strategies did not seem to develop until the seventh or eighth. Czentovic's pauses for thought were becoming longer; we sensed that the true battle for the upper hand had begun. But, to be perfectly honest, the gradual development of the game was something of a disappointment to us laymen, as that of any real game in a tournament would have been. For as the pieces wove themselves together into a strange decorative pattern, the actual state of play became increasingly impenetrable to us. We could not discern the intentions of either player or make out who had the advantage. We saw individual pieces moving like levers to pry open enemy lines, but, since everything these superior players did was always calculated several moves ahead, we were unable to grasp the strategic purpose of this give and take. Our lack of comprehension was gradually joined by a paralyzing fatigue, chiefly attributable to Czentovic's endless delays, by which our friend too began to be visibly irritated. I watched uneasily as the game went on and he fidgeted more and more in his chair, now nervously lighting one cigarette after another, now seizing a pencil to make a note of something. Then he ordered more mineral water, hurriedly downing glass after glass. It was obvious that he was calculating his moves a hundred times faster than Czentovic. Each time that Czentovic decided, after endless deliberation, to move a piece forward with his heavy hand, our friend only smiled, like someone seeing the arrival of something long expected, and was already responding. His racing mind must have calculated all his opponent's possible moves ahead of time; for the longer Czentovic drew out his decision, the more our friend's impatience grew, and as he waited his lips were pressed together in an expression of annoyance, almost hostility. But Czentovic was not to be rushed. He deliberated silently, doggedly, pausing at greater and greater length as the board emptied of pieces. At the forty-second move, after a solid two hours and forty-five minutes, we all sat around the table exhausted and almost indifferent. One of the ship's officers had already left; the other had taken out a book and did not glance up unless something changed. But then, as Czentovic was preparing to move, the unexpected suddenly happened. When Dr. B. saw Czentovic reaching out to advance his knight, he tensed like a cat about to pounce. His entire body began to tremble, and as soon as Czentovic had moved the knight he abruptly pushed his queen forward and in a loud and triumphant voice said, "So! Finished!" Dr. B. leaned back, folded his arms across his chest, and looked challengingly at Czentovic. His eyes were smoldering.

We couldn't help bending over the board to study this move, announced with such triumph. At first glance no direct threat could be seen; so our friend must have been referring to a development that we short-sighted amateurs could not yet calculate. Czentovic was the only one who had remained motionless in the face of this defiant pronouncement; he sat there as imperturbably as if he had completely missed the insulting "Finished!" Nothing happened. Involuntarily we all held our breaths, and suddenly you could hear the ticking of the clock on the table, put there to time the players. Three minutes passed, seven minutes, eight minutes—Czentovic did not move, but it seemed to me that his large nostrils were flaring still further from internal tension. This silent waiting seemed as unbearable to our friend as it did to us. He suddenly leapt to his feet and began to pace back and forth in the smoking lounge, first slowly, then ever faster. We all watched him with some amazement, but none with as much unease as I, for it struck me that his steps always measured out the same distance despite the intensity of his pacing; it was as though each time he ran up against an invisible barrier in the middle of the empty room, forcing him to reverse course. And I knew with a shiver that in his pacing he was unconsciously tracing the dimensions of his cell; during his months of incarceration he must have paced in just this way, like a caged animal, his hands clenched and his shoulders hunched precisely as they were now; this, just this, must have been the way he had walked up and down, thousands of times, the red light of madness in his blank, yet feverish gaze. But his mental powers still seemed to be entirely intact, for from time to time he

turned to the table impatiently to see if Czentovic
had reached a decision. Nine minutes, ten minutes
went by. Then at last something happened that none
of us had expected. Czentovic slowly raised his heavy
hand, which had been resting motionless on the
table. We were all eager to see what he would do. But
instead of making a move, he slowly and resolutely
swept the pieces off the board with the back of his
hand. It took us a moment to understand: Czentovic
had resigned. He had capitulated, so that we wouldn't
see him being checkmated. Improbably, the world
champion, the winner of countless tournaments, had
surrendered to an unknown, a man who had not
touched a chessboard for twenty or twenty-five years.
Our friend the nobody, the cipher, had defeated the
strongest chess player on earth in open battle!

In our excitement we had risen to our feet without
realizing it, one after another. All of us felt we had to
say or do something to express our joy and awe. The
only one who remained calm and still was Czentovic.
After a measured pause he lifted his head. He gazed
stonily at our friend.

"Another game?" he asked.

"Of course," Dr. B. replied with an enthusiasm
that I found disagreeable and, before I could remind
him of his resolution to content himself with a single
game, he immediately sat down and began to set up

the pieces again with feverish haste. His movements as he assembled them were so brusque that twice a pawn slipped through his trembling fingers to the floor; my nagging disquiet at the sight of his unnatural excitement had now grown into a kind of anxiety. For a visible exaltation had come over this man, previously so quiet and calm; the twitch at the corner of his mouth was more and more frequent, and his body shook as though in the grip of a sudden fever.

"No!" I whispered to him gently. "Not now! That's enough for one day! It's too much of a strain for you."

"A strain! Ha!" He gave a loud and nasty laugh. "I could have played seventeen games by this time instead of all this lollygagging! At this pace the only strain is staying awake!—Now then! Start, why don't you!"

His tone as he said these last words to Czentovic was fierce, almost coarse. Czentovic looked at him calmly and evenly, but something in his stony, unwavering gaze suggested a clenched fist. Suddenly there was something new between the two of them: a dangerous tension, a passionate hatred. They were no longer opponents testing their abilities in a spirit of play, but enemies resolved to annihilate each other. Czentovic delayed for a long time before making the first move. It was clear to me that this was intentional. The experienced tactician had evidently discovered that he was wearing his opponent down and setting him on edge by his very slowness. Thus it was some four minutes before he executed the most ordinary, the simplest of all openings, advancing his king's pawn two squares. Our friend immediately countered with his own king's pawn. Again Czentovic paused for an endless, almost unendurable time. It was like the moment after a great bolt of lightning: your heart pounds, you wait and wait, but the thunder never comes. He deliberated silently and with a slowness that, I was more and more certain, was malicious; in the meantime I observed Dr. B. He had just gulped down his third glass of water. I couldn't help recalling what he had told me about his feverish thirst in his cell. All the symptoms of abnormal excitation were clearly apparent; I saw the perspiration appear on his brow while the scar on his hand became redder and stood out more sharply than before. But he was still in control of himself. It was not until the fourth move, over which Czentovic was once again endlessly deliberating, that he lost his composure and suddenly barked:

"Come on, make your move!"

Czentovic looked up coolly. "As far as I know, we agreed on a move time of ten minutes. As a matter of principle I won't play with anything less."

Dr. B. bit his lip; I noticed that his foot was tapping more and more anxiously under the table, while I myself, with an oppressive premonition of some approaching outrage, was increasingly nervous. And at the eighth move there was in fact a second incident. Dr. B., who had been waiting with less and less self-control, was unable to maintain his composure; he fidgeted and unconsciously began to drum on the table with his fingers. Once more Czentovic raised his heavy peasant's head.

"May I ask you not to drum? It disturbs me. I can't play if you do that."

"Ha!" laughed Dr. B. "That's clear enough."

Czentovic's forehead flushed. "What do you mean by that?" he asked sharply and angrily.

Dr. B. gave another short, nasty laugh. "Nothing. Just that you're obviously very nervous."

Czentovic said nothing and lowered his head. It took him seven minutes to make his next move, and the game dragged on at this deadly pace. Czentovic seemed increasingly to be made of stone; eventually he was taking the maximum time before every move, while from one pause to the next our friend's behavior became ever more bizarre. He no longer seemed to be taking part in the game: he was involved in something quite different. He had left off his excited pacing and sat motionless in his chair. Staring before him with a vacant, almost crazed expression, he murmured incomprehensible words to himself in a continuous stream; either he was engrossed in an endless calculation of moves, or else (this was my deepest suspicion) he was working out entirely different games, for whenever Czentovic at last made a move, he had to be brought back to an awareness of his surroundings. Then it always took him a few moments to reorient himself; I was beginning to suspect that he had actually long since forgotten Czentovic and the rest of us in this quiet madness, which seemed ready to explode into violence of some kind. And, at the nineteenth move, the crisis in fact erupted. Czentovic had no sooner made his move than Dr. B. abruptly pushed his bishop forward three squares with barely a glance at the board and shouted so loudly that we all jumped:

"Check! Your king is in check!"

We immediately looked at the board, expecting an out-of-the-way move. But none of us was prepared for what happened a moment later. Czentovic raised his head very, very slowly and looked at each of us in turn (he had never done this). He seemed to be relishing something immensely, for gradually a pleased and distinctly mocking smile came to his lips. Only after he had savored to the full this triumph, still incomprehensible to us, did he address himself to our group with feigned politeness.

"Excuse me—but I see no check. Does one of the gentlemen perhaps see how my king is in check?"

We looked at the board, then uneasily at Dr. B. Czentovic's king was in fact completely protected from the bishop by a pawn (a child could have seen it), and could not possibly be in check. We were troubled. Had our friend in his excitement moved to the wrong square? Alerted by our silence, Dr. B. too now stared at the board and began to stammer violently:

"But the king should be on f7... That's wrong, where it is, completely wrong. You made the wrong move! Everything's in the wrong place on this board... The pawn should be on g5, not on g4... This is a different game... This is..."

Suddenly he broke off. I had taken him firmly by the arm, or rather clamped his arm so hard that, even in his feverish confusion, he had to feel my grip. He turned and stared at me like a sleepwalker.

"What... what do you want?"

I said simply, "Remember!," and drew my finger over the scar on his hand. He followed my movement without meaning to, and his eyes stared glassily at the blood-red line. Then he began suddenly to shake, and a shudder passed over his entire body.

"My God," he whispered, his lips pale. "Have I said or done something wrong... Am I in trouble again?"

"No," I whispered gently. "But you must end the game immediately, it's high time. Remember what the doctor told you!"

Dr. B. stood up immediately. "Please forgive my foolish error," he said in his former polite tone and bowed to Czentovic. "What I said was of course pure nonsense. Needless to say, it's your game." He then turned to us. "I must also beg pardon of the gentlemen. But I warned you at the outset not to expect too much. I am sorry to have made a fool of myself—this is the last time I will try my hand at chess."

He bowed and departed as unassumingly and mysteriously as he had first appeared. I alone knew why this man would never again touch a chessboard, while the others were left a little confused, with the vague feeling that they had barely escaped something awkward and dangerous. McConnor was disappointed. "Damned fool!" he growled. Czentovic, the last to rise from his chair, glanced again at the half-finished game.

"Pity," he said generously. "The attack was not at all poorly conceived. For an amateur, this gentleman is really extraordinarily talented."

TITLES IN SERIES